W9-BFW-622

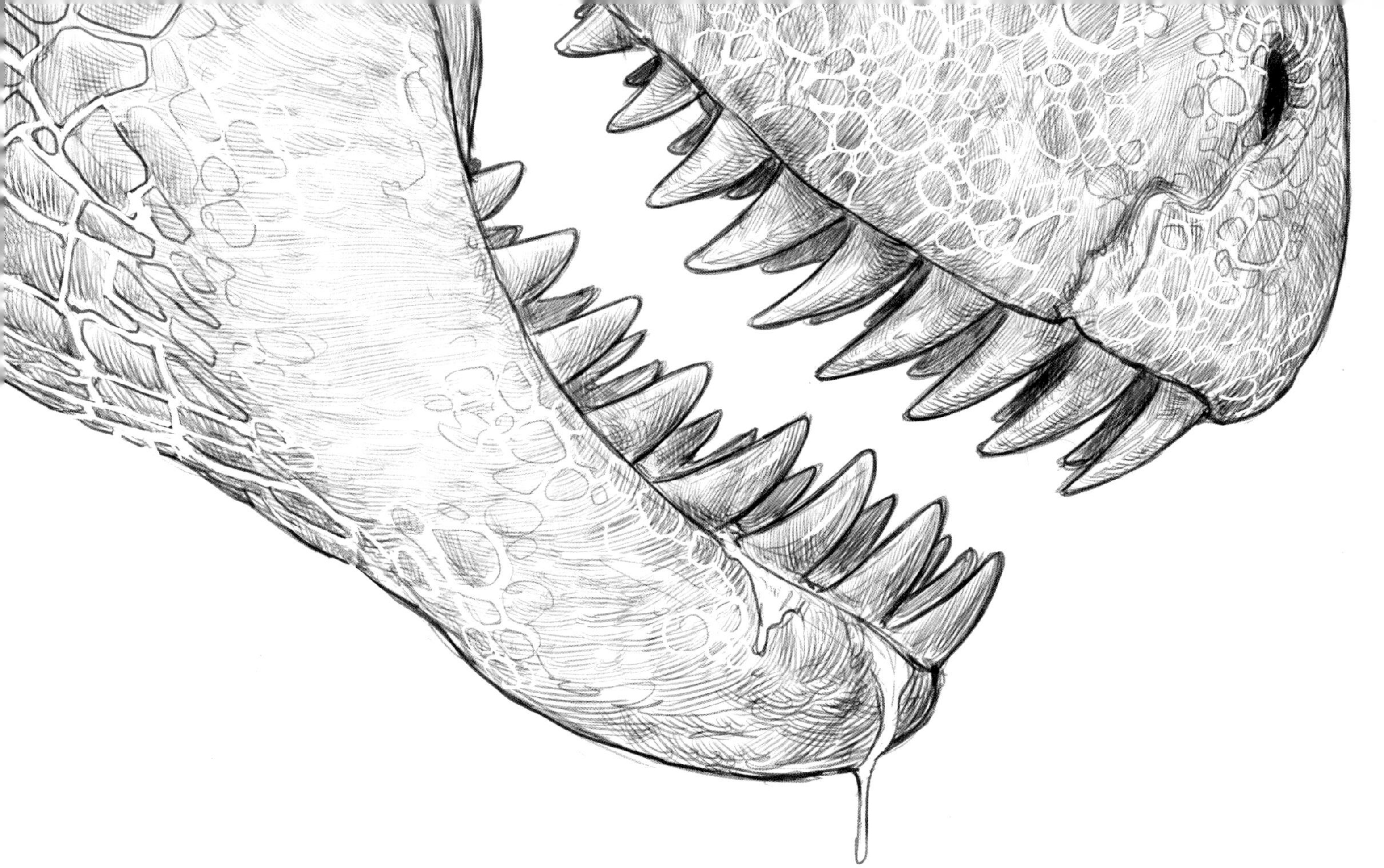

THE DINOSAUR

Frédéric Brrémaud

Federico Bertolucci

www.MAGNETIC-PRESS.com

For Émilie Bob, Alix Patafix, and Arsène la Baleine...
Frédéric Brrémaud

For Francesca, Alice, and Vanda.
Federico Bertolucci

"I BECOME QUITE MELANCHOLY AND DEEPLY GRIEVED TO SEE MEN BEHAVE TO EACH OTHER AS THEY DO. EVERYWHERE I FIND NOTHING BUT BASE FLATTERY, INJUSTICE, SELF-INTEREST, DECEIT, AND ROGUERY."

THE MISANTHROPE - ACT ONE, SCENE ONE
MOLIÈRE, 1666

IN THE ANIMAL KINGDOM, ANIMALS NEITHER LOVE NOR HATE EACH OTHER.

LOVE AND HATE ARE PARTS OF A NATURAL WHOLE. A SUPREME BALANCE MANY CONSIDER TO BE UNIVERSAL, OR EVEN DIVINE. AN ELEMENTAL LOVE.

A LOVE THAT MANKIND COULD NEVER EXPERIENCE.

The LOVE series has been recognized for the following awards :
- LUCCA 2011 (Italy) - *Prix spécial du jury*
- ANGOULÊME 2012 (France) - *Sélection Prix BD des Collégiens*
- YALSA 2015 (USA) - *Selection Great Graphic Novels for Teens*
- IPPY AWARDS 2016 (USA) - *Gold Medal: Best Graphic Novel*
- EISNER AWARDS 2016 (USA) - *Federico Bertolucci: Best Painter/Multi-media artist (nominee)*

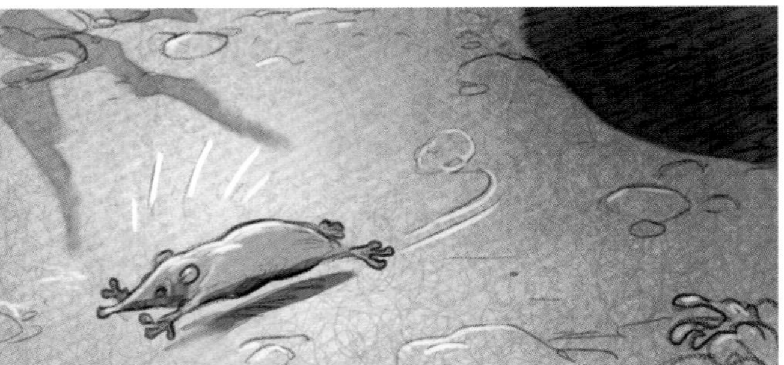

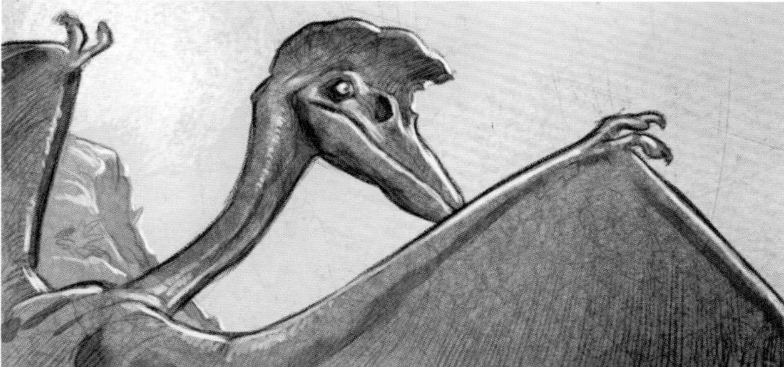

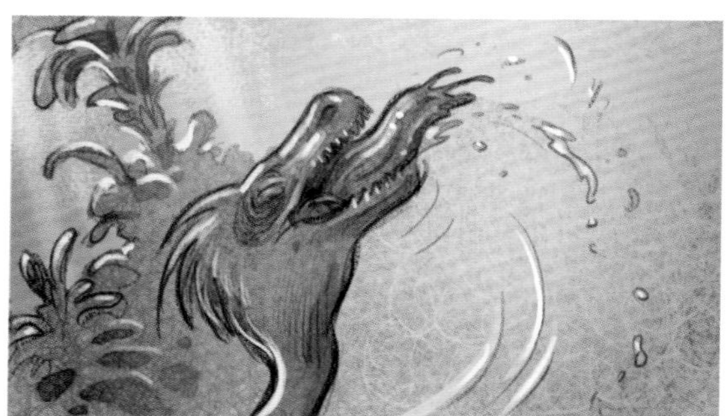

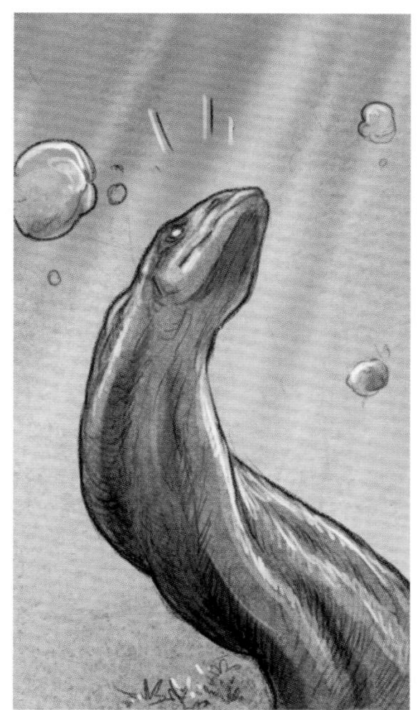

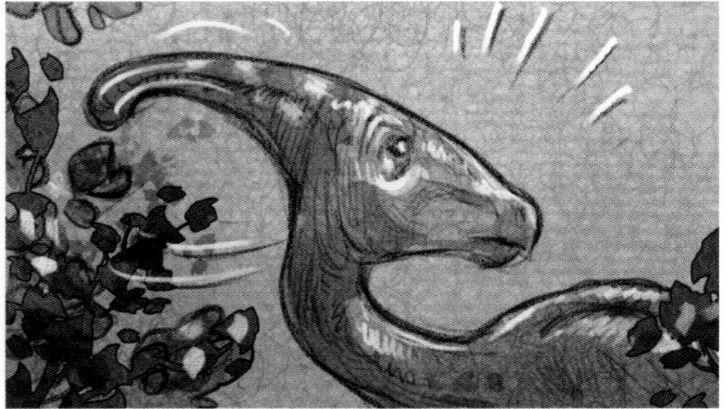

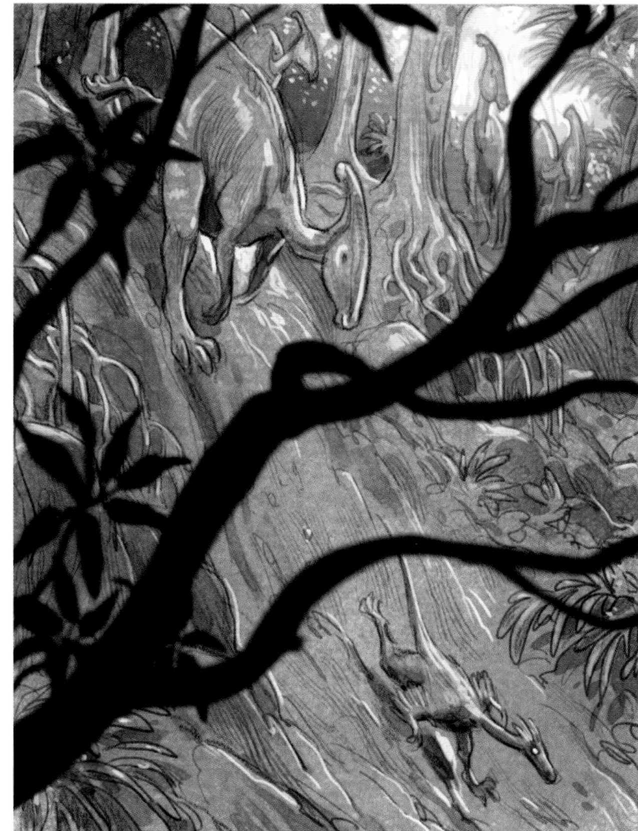

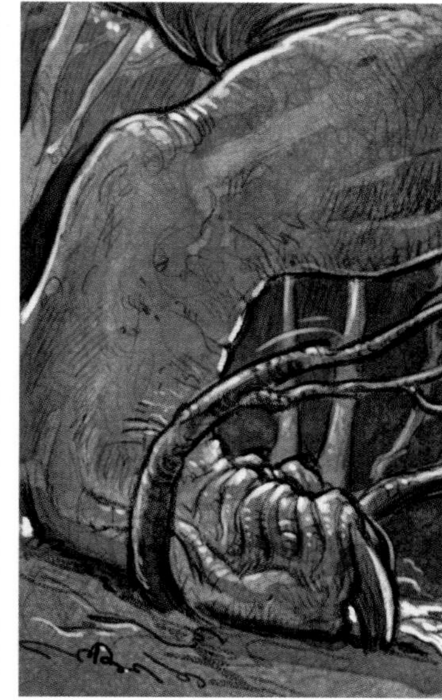

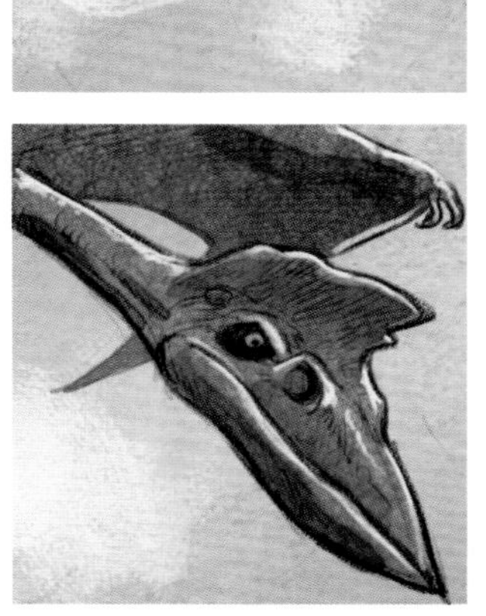
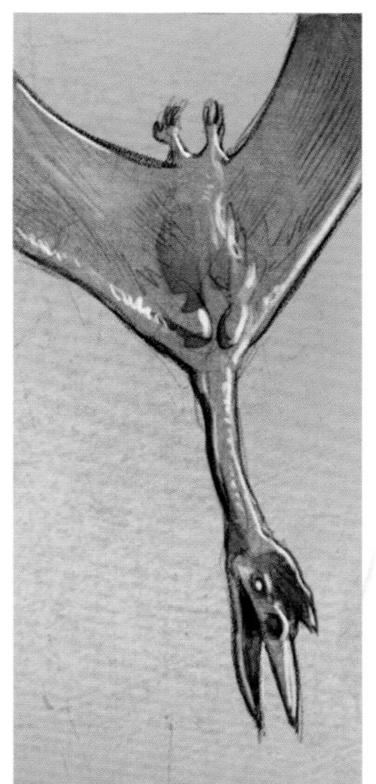

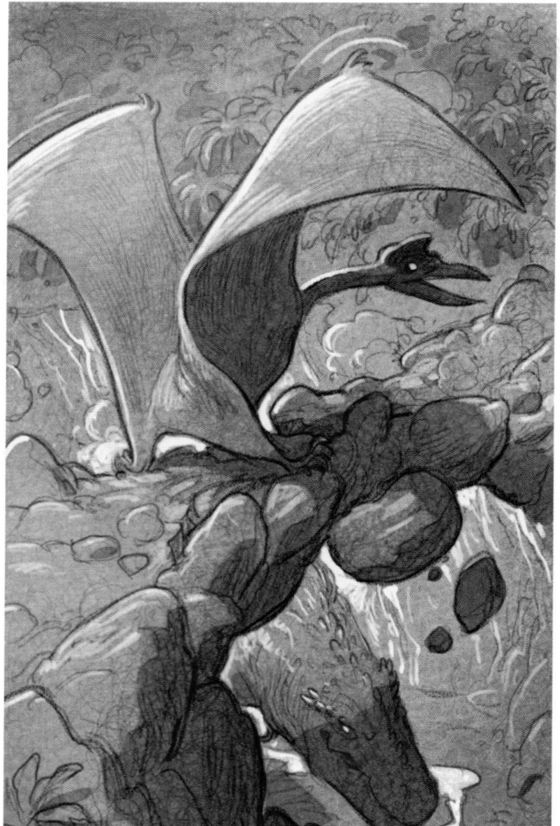

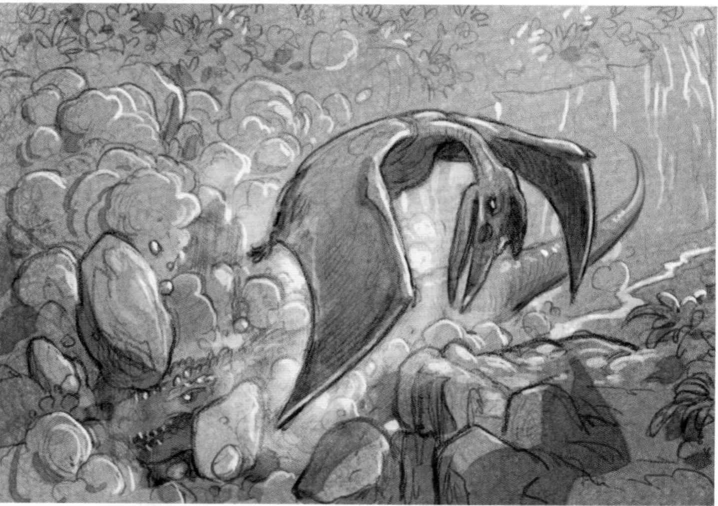

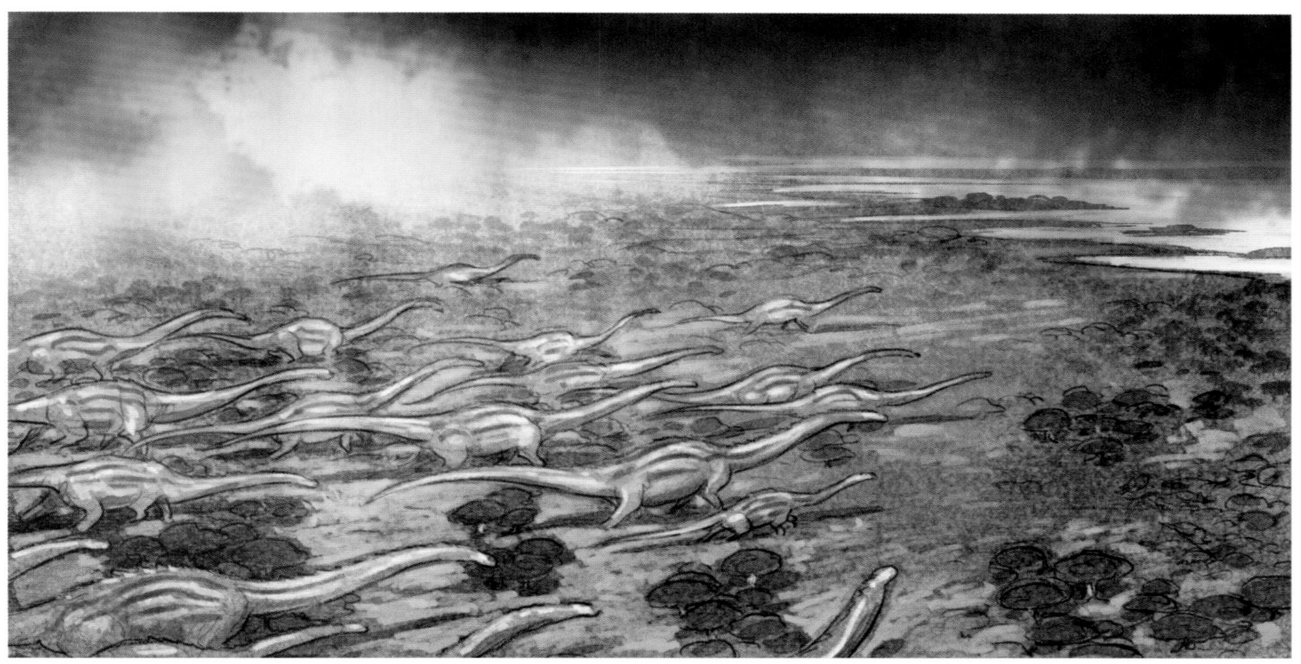

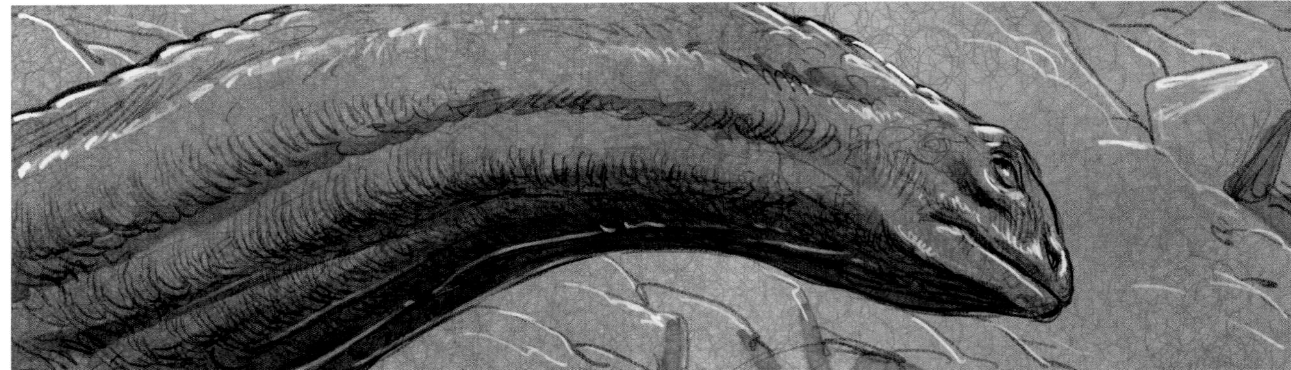

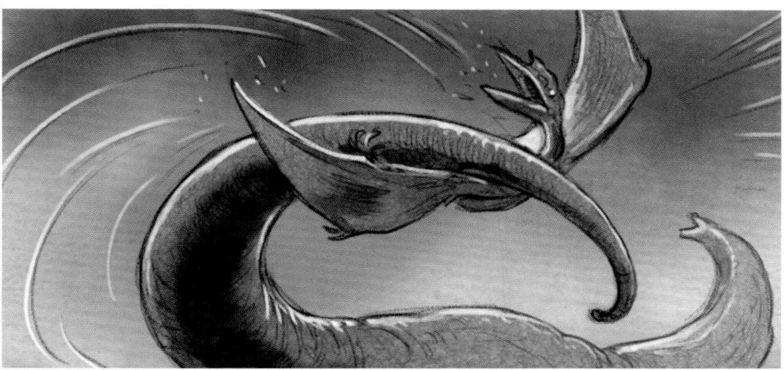

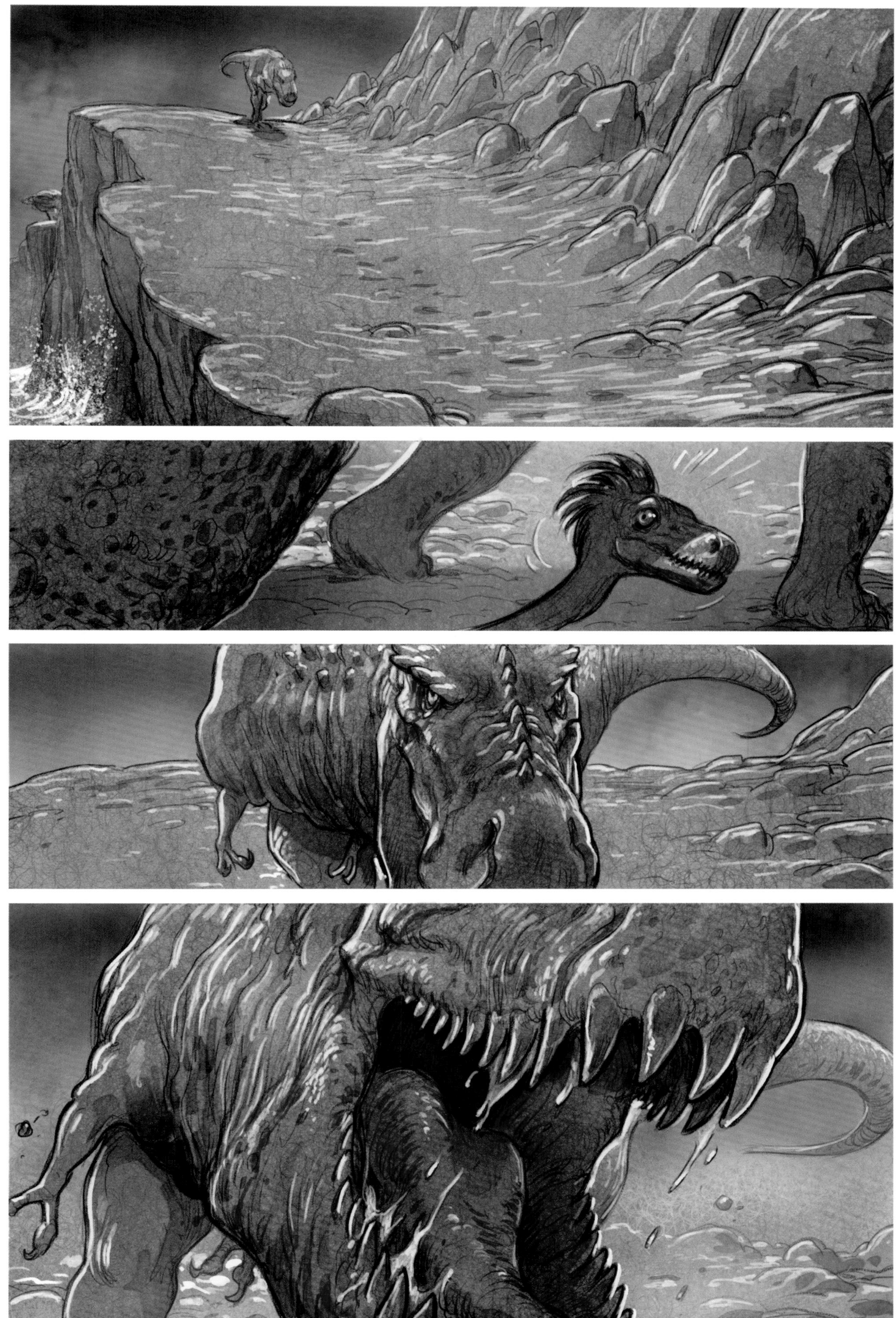

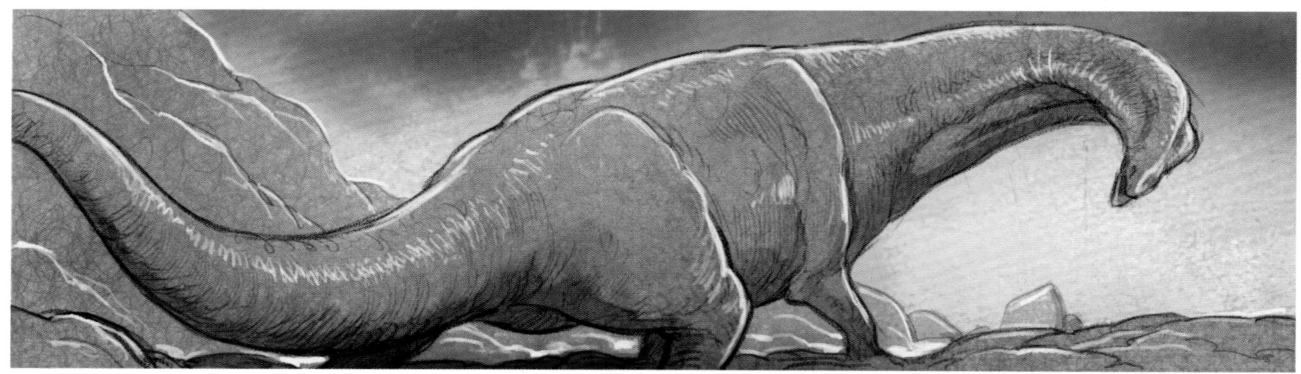

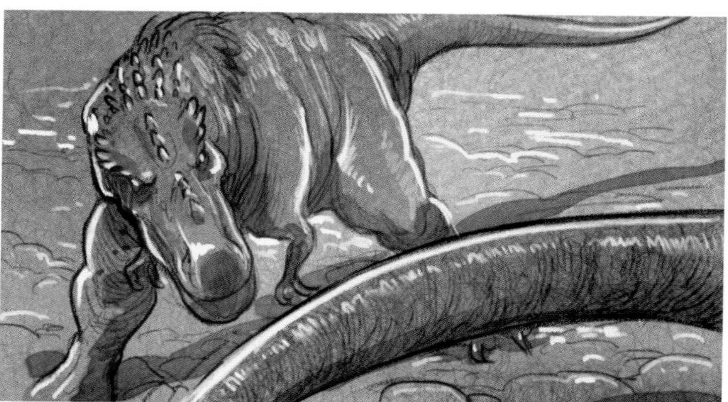

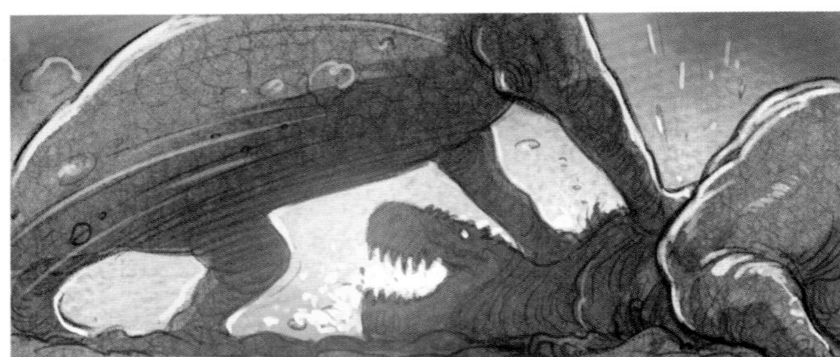

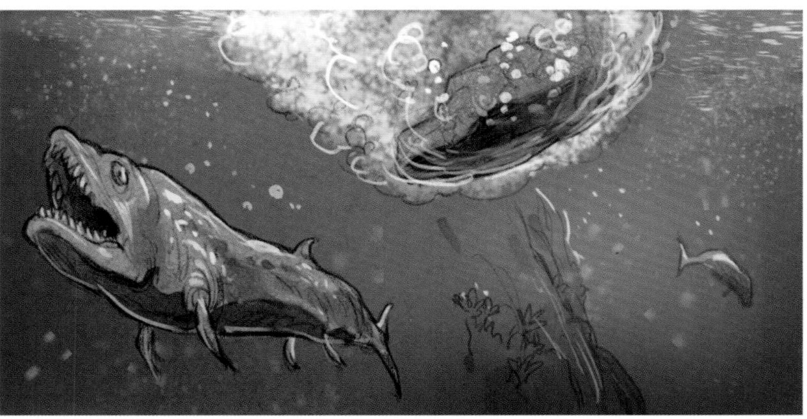

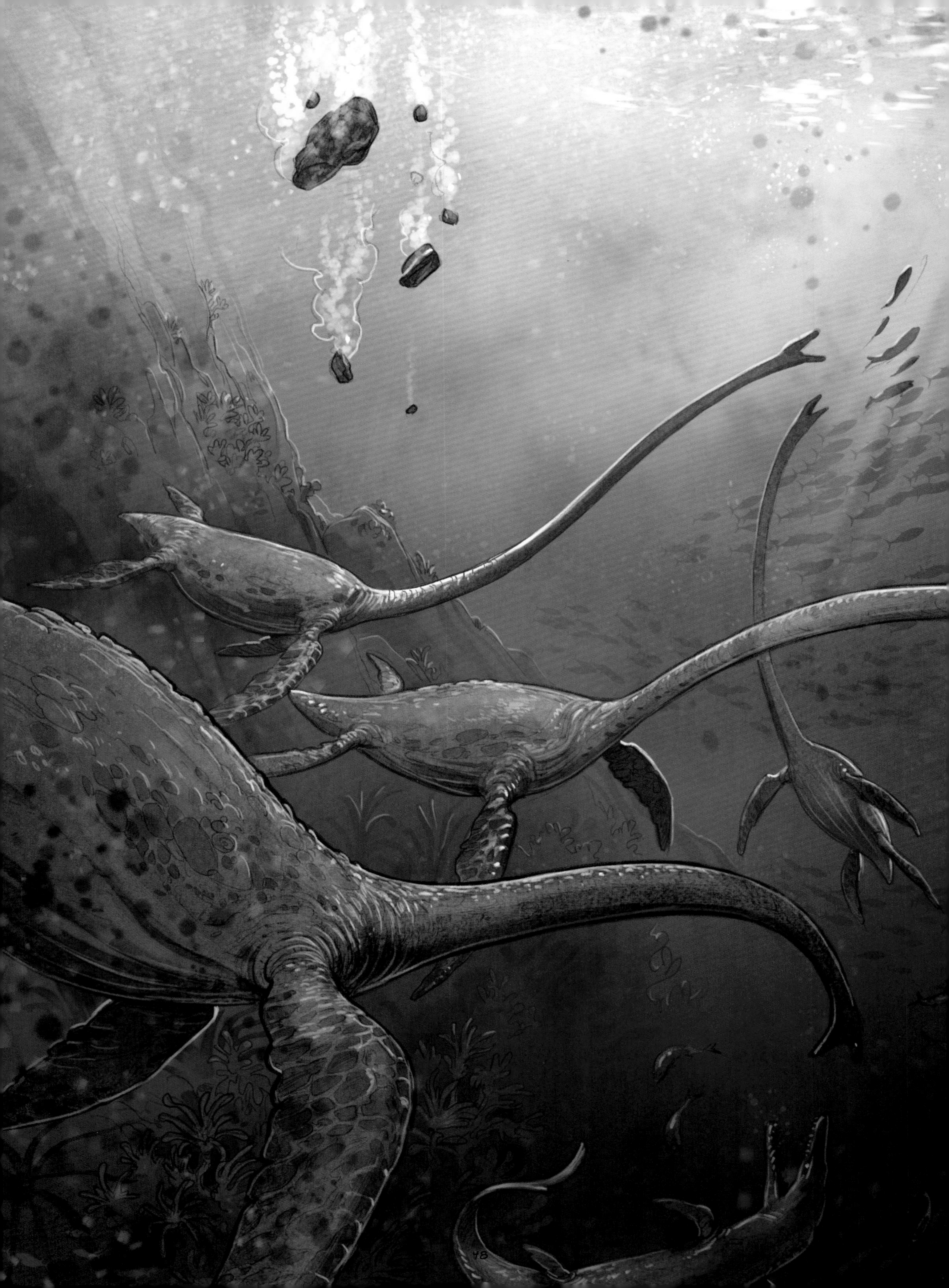

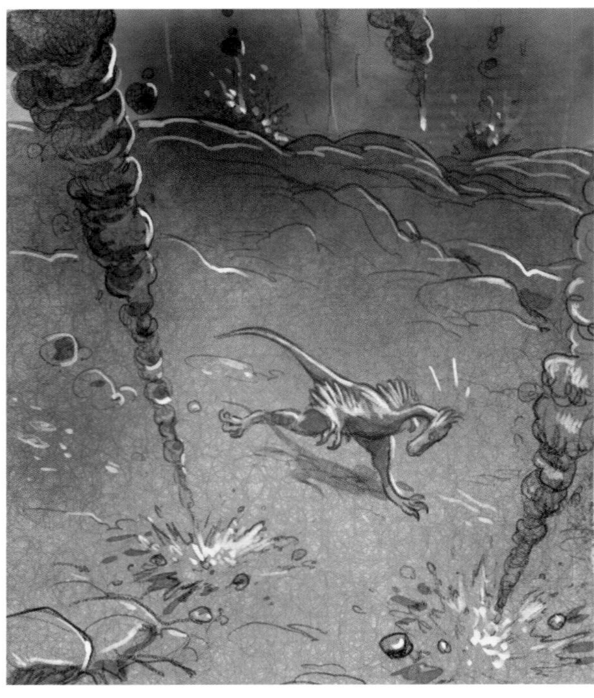

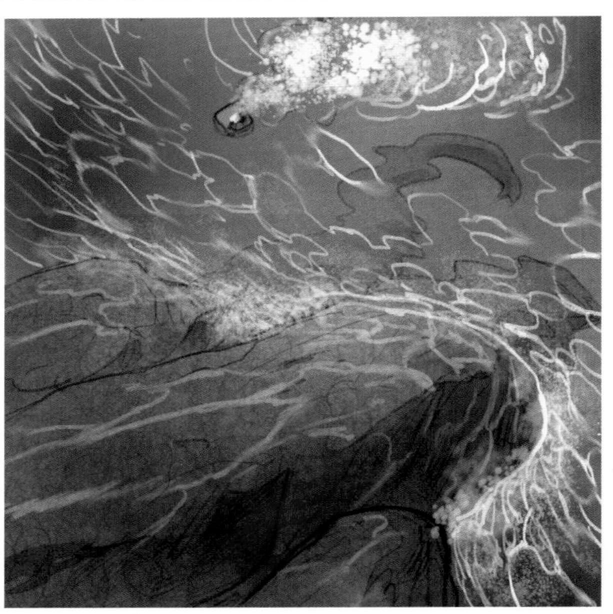

love
ART
Bambiraptor
Feinbergi

Spinosaurus Aegyptiacus

Carnotaurus
Sastrei

Tyrannosaurus
Rex

Stegosaurus
Tyrannosaurus Rex

Lexovisaurus
Durobrivensis
Stegosaurus

Isisaurus
Colberti

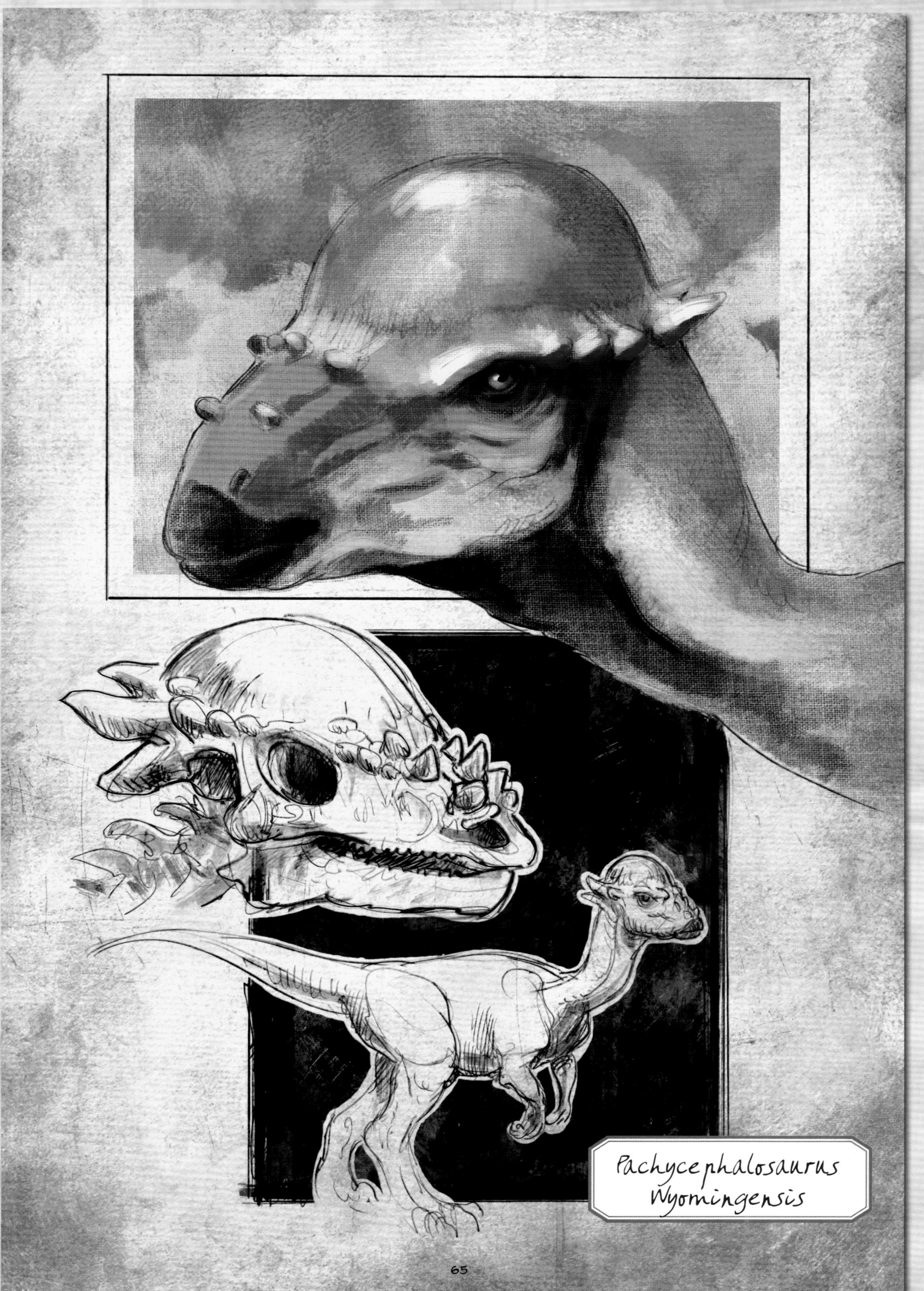
Pachycephalosaurus
Wyomingensis

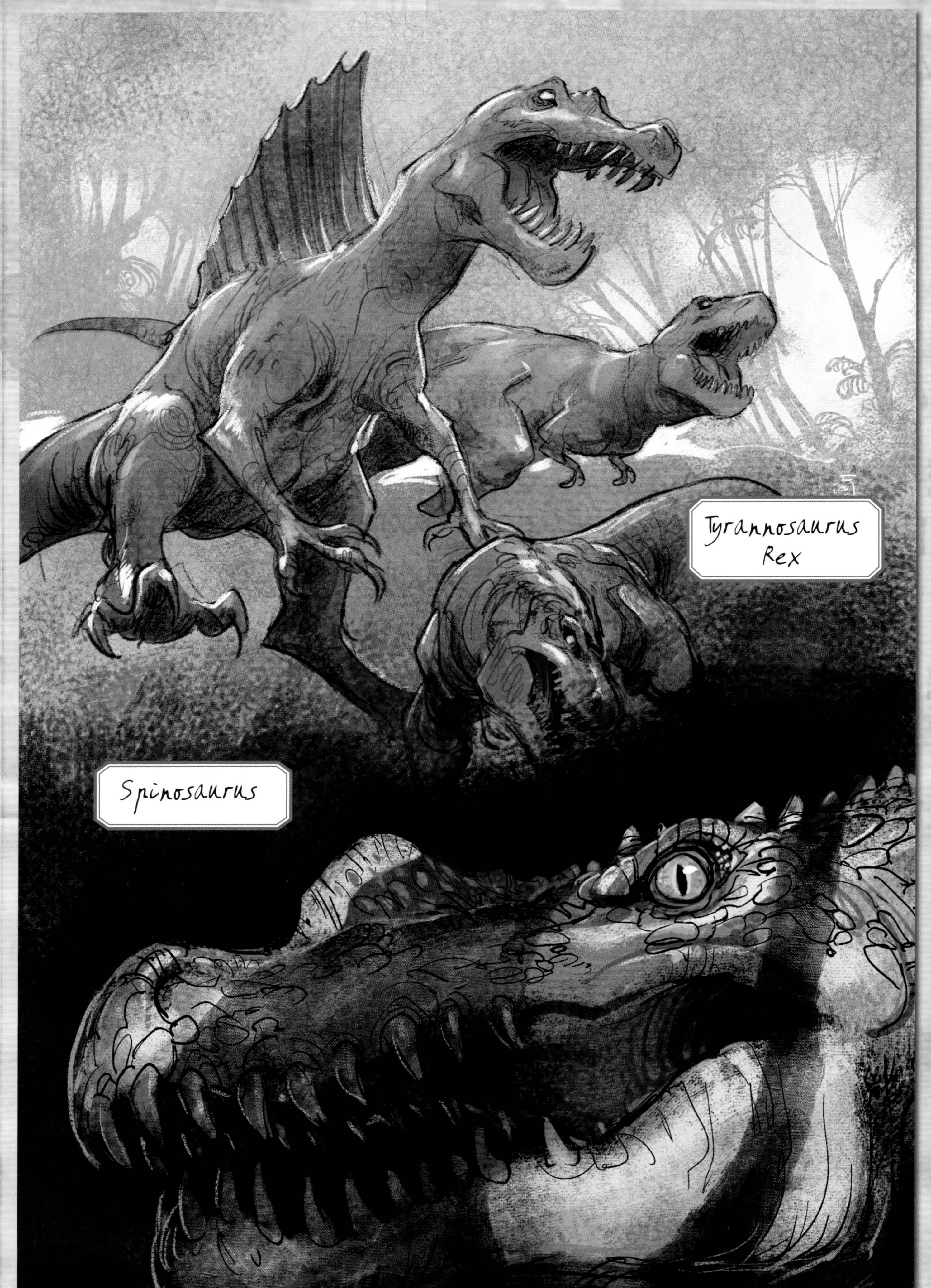

Tyrannosaurus Rex
Spinosaurus

Amargasaurus Cazaui

Nigersaurus Taqueti

Ultrasauros Macintoshi

Argentinosaurus Huinculensis

Cnetochasma

Dilophosaurus Wetherilli
Coelophysis Bauri

Triceratops
Horridus

Styracosaurus

Chasmosaurus

Centrosaurus

Quetzalcoatlus

Deinocheirus
Mirificus

Bambiraptor Feinbergi

Dimetrodon

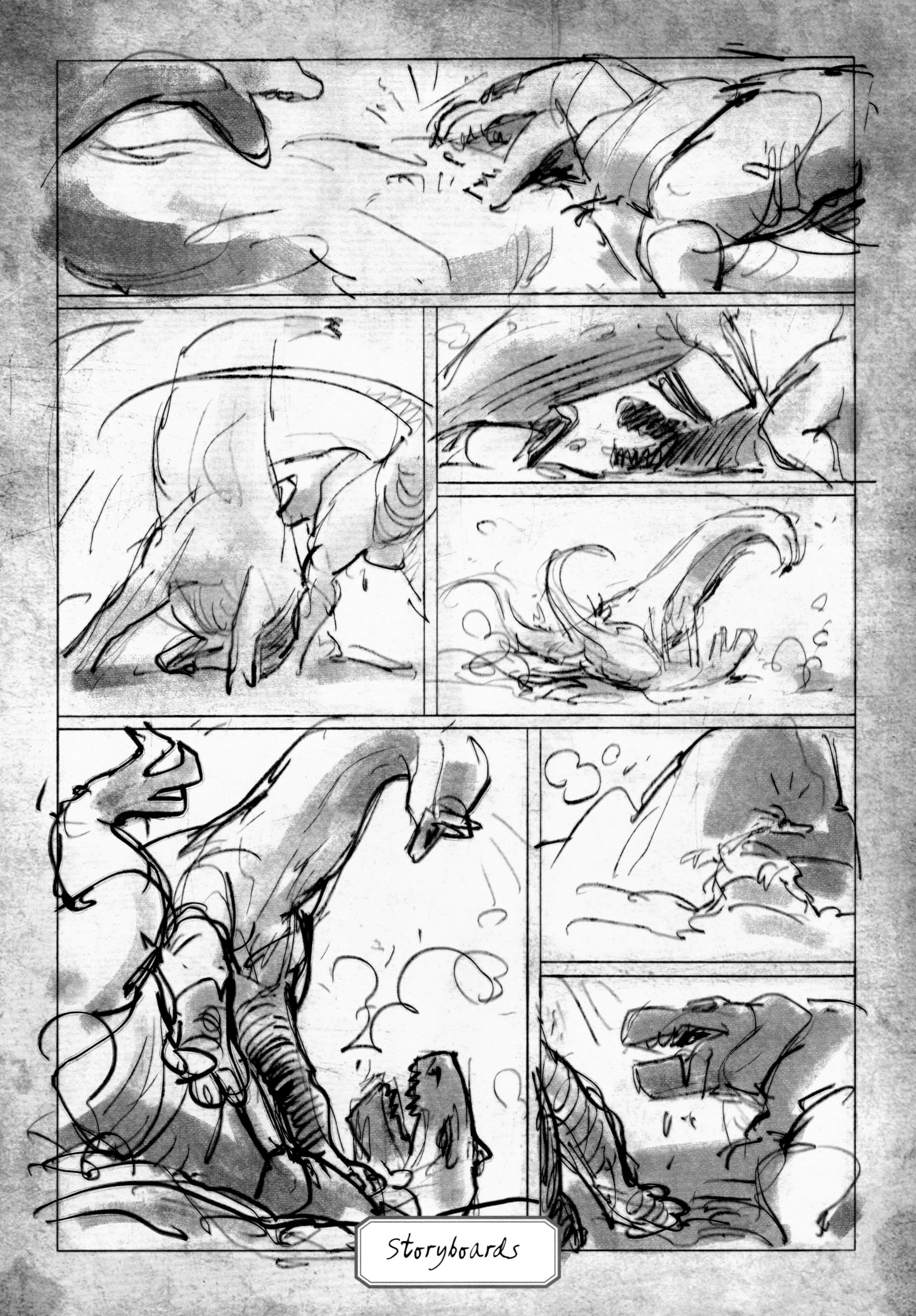

Storyboards

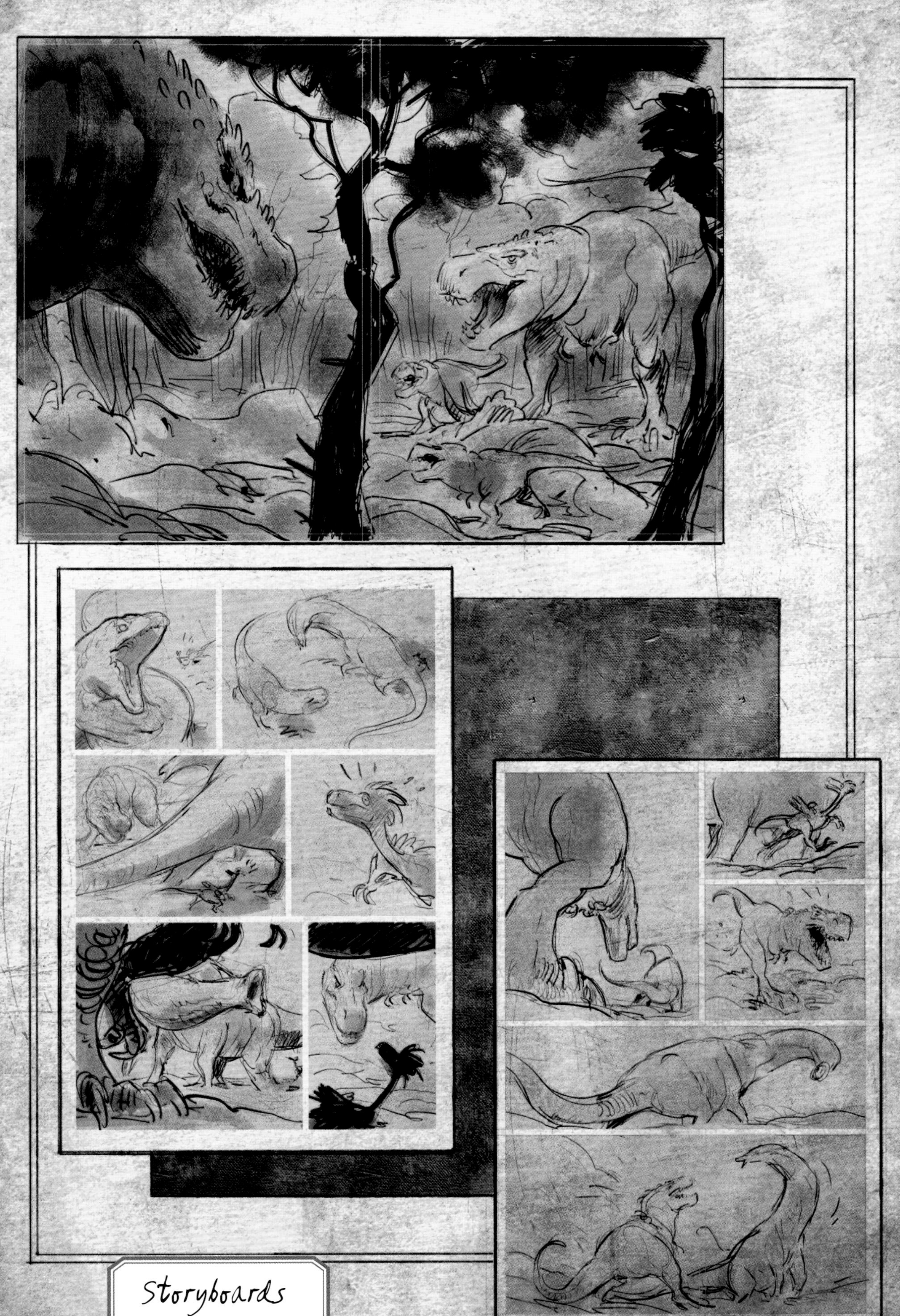

Storyboards

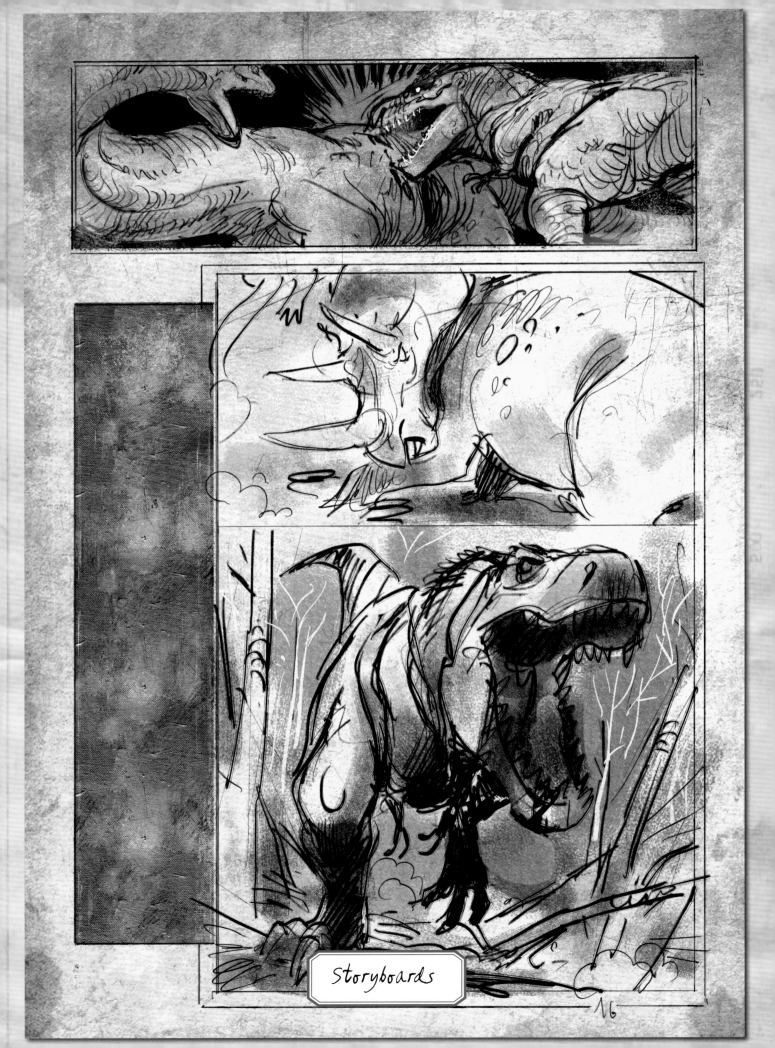

Storyboards

Cover Sketches

Written by **Frédéric Brrémaud**
Illustrated by **Federico Bertolucci**

Logo Design by : **Tony Derbomez**

MAGNETIC PRESS
Mike Kennedy, *Publisher / President*
Wes Harris, *CEO*
David Dissanayake, *Marketing & PR*
4910 N. Winthrop Ave #3S
Chicago, IL 60640
WWW.MAGNETIC-PRESS.COM

ALSO AVAILABLE:

LOVE volume 1 THE TIGER

LOVE volume 2 THE FOX

LOVE volume 3 THE LION

LOVE volume 4: THE DINOSAUR
Original Graphic Novel Hardcover
January 2017. FIRST PRINTING
ISBN: 978-1-942367-36-9